THE ALIEN ADVENTURES OF FINN CASPIAN

THE ACCIDENTAL VOLCANO

Read more of Finn Caspian's
alien adventures!

THE ALIEN ADVENTURES OF FINN CASPIAN

THE ACCIDENTAL VOLCANO

Jonathan Messinger

Illustrated by Aleksei Bitskoff

HARPER

An Imprint of HarperCollinsPublishers

For Griffin and Emerson

CONTENTS

A Note About This Story

The tale you are about to read takes place approximately **36.54372 million miles away** from Earth, as the crow flies. It has been collected and woven together via various interview transcripts, recordings, and interstellar **laser screams** sent to Earth from the *Famous Marlowe 280 Interplanetary Exploratory Space Station* over the past decade.

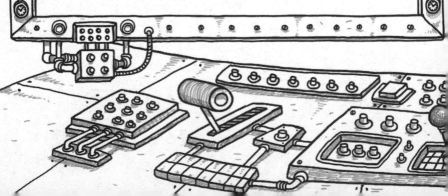

"Laser scream" may be a new term for you, as it is still not well understood on Earth, but we don't have time to get into it here.

The astronauts who boarded the *Marlowe* were charged with **one mission: to discover a planet where humans could one day live**. Captain Isabel Caspian sends out teams of explorers. Finn and his friends are all remarkable, but Finn will always have a special place in the history books.

Because Finn was the first kid born in space.

So in many ways, Finn was born for exactly the type of situation in which we find him here in this book. But it will be up to you to decide if that makes him lucky or not.

HALL OF
EXPLORERS

Abigail
Obaro

Troop 301 Captain

Finn
Caspian

Chief Detective

Chief Technologist

Sergeant-at-Arms

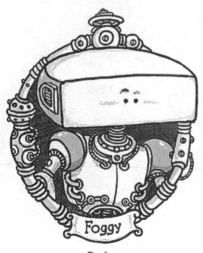

Robot

Little Sister

Chapter One
Breaking Bread

Finn crouched low beneath the table in the corner of the room. He wedged himself as deeply as he could into the shadows. He held his breath. There was no sign of anyone yet, but he knew they were out there. Did they know he was in here? If they did, he was a sitting duck.

He saw boots in the doorway. But were they friend boots or foe boots?

Finn let out the tiniest breath and inhaled again.

"In here. I heard something," said the voice in the hallway. Definitely not a friend voice.

The boots ran inside, followed by another pair.

"I know I heard something," said the voice again. "Check the closet."

The closet was on the other side of the room. Finn saw both pairs of boots walk toward it.

Now was his chance. He could surprise his enemies from behind or try to run for the door. Fight or flight. Stay or run away. Battle or . . . something that rhymes with battle. This was no time for poetry!

The invaders opened the closet. Finn snuck out from beneath the table and bolted for the door. The enemies turned, and Finn heard the sound of a laser.

"Pew! Pew!"

He leapt through the door into the hallway. The enemy's laser buzzed so close to Finn's ear, he could feel the wind of it passing by his head. The wall in front of him exploded. With bread crumbs—flaky, buttery bread crumbs. A croissant slammed into the wall, bounced once, and settled onto the floor. Finn kept running.

Laser tag aboard a space station is intense. It's both playtime and combat training. Except, because like everywhere in the universe, parents make a lot of boring rules, Finn and his friends couldn't use actual lasers. So they just said "pew pew." And without any other equipment, they snuck whatever stale dinner rolls were left over from the night before and threw them at each other. So technically it was bread tag.

And Finn was a bread-tag ninja.

"How did you miss him?!" he heard Abigail yell behind him.

"It's not my fault!" shouted Vale. "Who serves croissants for dinner?!"

Abigail and Vale versus Finn and Elias.

Finn was now a good ten seconds ahead of the other team. He booked it down the corridor, trying to remember whose compartment Elias was hiding in. This was the plan. Finn would distract Abigail and Vale while Elias worked on his ultimate invention: a breadshield.

He came to a door.

"Bingo," he said.

He pressed the button and opened the door

to the compartment where Elias's family lived.

Elias was sitting on the floor of his bedroom surrounded by about eight hundred wires, batteries, nodes, and other electronics. Finn didn't know what half of them did.

"Elias?" said Finn. "You're not done?!"

"No!" said Elias. "Almost. Or, I was almost done. And then I started working on this robot I've been messing with."

Elias held up a small robot, slightly larger than the croissant Finn had dodged. It did not look even remotely near finished.

"Why are you working on that?!" shouted Finn. "Abigail and Vale are right behind me! Where's the breadshield?"

"It's over there!" said Elias. He waved his arms over all the pieces lying on the floor. "I mean, it will be over there. I just need ten minutes to fix something on this robot, and then I can build the breadshield."

"Pew."

Finn felt the unmistakable thud of a croissant hitting him in the back.

"Pew."

A French roll flew over Finn's shoulder and landed in Elias's lap.

Elias picked it up and bit off the corner.

"It's going to be really cool," he said, his mouth full of stale bread. "Like, I think it's a completely different kind of robot than anyone has—"

"Game over, Elias!" said Finn.

"Oh," said Elias. "My bad."

"Your bad, my good," said Vale.

"That is barely English," said Abigail. She and Vale walked out into the corridor. "But! I won't argue with you since we. Are. CHAMPIONS!"

The two took off down the hallway, celebrating.

"Sorry, Finn," said Elias.

Finn sat down on the floor.

"It's okay," he said. "It's just laser tag. But next time, maybe be a little quicker?"

"I know," said Elias. "But it's hard to be in the middle of the action when all I want to do is build things. I can't work at light speed."

"Bread speed," said Finn. "And it's fine—we're a solid team."

"A solid team that has lost seven times in a row," said Elias.

Finn shrugged. He picked up a wire and a piece of metal that looked like a hamburger.

"So do I put this hoozit in that whatzit?" he asked.

"Ha ha," said Elias. "It's okay. You catch up to them—I want to work on this."

"You sure?" said Finn.

"Yeah," said Elias. He looked down at the robot in his hands. "And I promise, next laser tag sesh, I won't let you down."

Finn ran out into the hallway, but Elias was so fixated on his robot he didn't notice.

"Well," said Elias. "I might let you down. I mean, I'll try not to. But sometimes I don't know if I can—oh, and you're not here anymore."

Chapter Two
Lights, Camera, Inaction

It didn't take long for Finn to catch up with Abigail and Vale. Abigail, the captain of Explorers Troop 301, looked over Finn's shoulder as he approached.

"No Elias?" she asked. "Hiding in shame after your defeat?"

"Nah," said Finn. "He's working on a new robot."

Elias was the chief technologist of Explorers Troop 301. He and his friends went out to explore all kinds of planets, and Elias did his best to create inventions that would help them.

"Oh," said Abigail. "You mean the one that's supposed to be able to identify whether an alien bug is poisonous right away?"

"No," said Finn. "Not that one."

"The one that can supposedly turn mud into food?"

"I don't think so," said Finn.

"The one that dances in five hundred different languages?"

Finn laughed. "No," he said. "Elias said it was a brand-new type of robot. Something no one had thought of yet."

Vale, the explorer troop's sergeant-at-arms, didn't say anything. Instead, he did his new signature move: a triple-double-dutch-flip-somersault-jump-sidekick-with-a-smile. Or at

least, in his mind, that was what he did. What he actually did looked more like a fish hailing a taxi.

"Nailed it!" Vale yelled. Abigail and Finn stopped walking and stared at their friend. "You're speechless! I knew it! Totally nailed it!"

"Kudos, Vale!" chirped Foggy, Finn's best bud and robot. Foggy was always up for anything and always very supportive of his human friends. It was how he was wired.

"I'm sure Elias will catch up with us in a second," said Finn. "He said he just needed to fix one thing."

But it would be a while before Elias caught up with them. Back in his compartment, he was in the zone, working on his robot. When he and his friends were out on missions, Elias wasn't the quickest thinker or the fastest on his feet. It never bothered his friends, but it bothered Elias.

He wanted to make something that would change all that. He held up the small robot he had been working on and smiled. It was almost done.

"You're my best idea yet," Elias said to the small bot.

And when Elias had an idea, he only needed four things: time to think, peace and quiet, chocolate chocolate-chip cookies, and a fire extinguisher, just in case.

But mostly he needed the cookies.

And the fire extinguisher.

Actually, forget the cookies. He really just needed the fire extinguisher.

Because the robot he'd been secretly making in his bedroom had caught fire.

Chapter Three
Robotics 101

The engineers of the *Marlowe 280* built all the robots in the robot room. It was a special place, specifically designed for making new mechanical friends. The engineers needed everything to be completely clean to do their work. One stray clump of dirt, and a robot's sensitive electronics could be ruined. Because it needed to stay so clean, it was one of the few rooms on the *Marlowe* where kids couldn't go without a parent.

That's why Elias kept a miniature laboratory in his bedroom. If he couldn't get to the robot room, he'd make a space to explore his ideas.

Normally, all the *Marlowe* robots got their personalities from a book. Once a robot was complete, its owner downloaded a book onto its hard drive. The robot then acted like a character in that book.

Finn's robot, Foggy, came from an adventure book. Genevieve Brooks, one of the older kids, had a robot named Sir Lance-a-bot. Legend had it that a Bilbot Baggins had once roamed the *Marlowe*'s hallways.

But Elias thought it would be fun to try a different way. He wanted to make a robot that had its own personality. No books. So he'd hidden a few parts in his room. And slowly but surely he'd built a small robot. It was the size of a skinny gerbil.

It would be the skinny gerbil that would change the universe.

Everything was perfect. All he had to do was press a button to start it up. Elias took a deep breath and powered it on.

And that's when it caught fire.

The fire alarm on the *Marlowe* was louder than a cat whose tail had just been stepped on. Elias didn't panic, but he did get up and walk out of his bedroom. He stood, waiting, in the living room. He knew the little fire-extinguishing robots were on their way. They looked like ketchup bottles on wheels. They would roll into his room, raise their tiny hoses, and shoot foam at the fire.

And then he would have to explain to his parents why he'd built a secret robot. But for now, all he had to do was wait. He just had to wait for the itty-bitty, teeny-tiny robots to roll in. Just wait and—

"OUT OF THE WAY, EVERYONE. I AM HERE. I AM SAVING THE DAY. THANK ME!"

A massive, shiny robot burst into the living room and past Elias, rushing to his bedroom. It looked down at the fire. Elias waited for it to shoot foam out of its hose, but nothing happened. The robot looked at Elias, then looked at the gerbil robot flaming at the foot of his bed.

"Well, aren't you going to put it out?" shouted Elias.

"SURE AM!" shouted the tall robot. It looked around the room.

"Do you have any foam?" said Elias.

"NOPE!" said the robot. "NO PROBLEM!"

And the tall, strange robot picked up its right foot and stomped on Elias's gerbilbot.

"FIXED!" shouted the robot, and it turned to leave. "I FIXED IT. I'M AWESOME."

"That was not awesome!" said Elias. "That was . . . that was . . . that was my robot!

Just then, Elias's parents and a handful of other engineers raced into his compartment.

"Elias, what happened? Are you okay?!" said his mother. She waved away the smoke and gave him a hug.

"Yeah," he said. "I tried to build a robot, and it caught fire. That chucklehead stepped on it." He pointed at the tall robot. "Who is that?"

"That's Voltronix Zu!" said his mother. "Our newest invention."

"He seems kind of . . ," Elias trailed off. He paused for a moment and tried to think of the right word. He looked at the tall robot. It was now literally patting itself on the back. "Dumb?"

"Oh, he just has a few kinks to work out," said his dad. "He's the first robot we made with its own brain. No books!"

Elias was shocked. That's what he had been working on.

"How?" asked Elias. "No. You didn't. I did. What? No. How?"

He was stuck in a loop.

Elias's dad looked down at the remains of the robot. He laughed.

"You know, son, you're supposed to build something, not destroy it."

He gave Elias a hug to show that he was just kidding.

"What is this pile of smoking metal, anyway?" asked his dad.

"Nothing," he said. "Just a dumb idea I had."

Chapter Four
A New Scope

Over the next few days, Elias's friends tried to cheer him up. They were getting ready to go on a mission to another planet. They were pretty sure this one wouldn't explode. Maybe.

But Elias kept thinking about the robot that had caught fire in his bedroom. At breakfast in the *Marlowe*'s great hall, he doodled more versions of it.

"Forget about the gerbilbot," said Finn. "Think of it as a controlled burn. You know, like we learned in science class? Like when you're trying to get rid of weeds. Sometimes you burn them on purpose so they can't come back."

"Yeah, but the robot wasn't a weed," said Elias. "And the burn was out of control!"

"No," said Vale. "The bad ideas are the weeds. And the fire on your carpet is, um, I don't know. That was just a fire, I guess."

"No more fires!" said Finn's mother, the captain of the *Marlowe*, as she strode into the great hall. She had come to tell them about their next mission.

"There won't be any surprises this time," she said. "I promise."

She told the explorers they were traveling to a planet with no threats. In fact, there were no aliens at all. There were plenty of plants and what looked like running rivers. But the

Marlowe's scientists had scanned the entire surface and not seen a single animal. Captain Caspian left to get her own breakfast.

"It sounds kind of boring," said Elias after she'd left. He stirred his cereal with rehydrated milk but didn't actually eat. "What's the point of going to a planet that doesn't have life?"

"Because," said Abigail, "it looks a lot like Earth. The adults think it has everything humans need to live: oxygen, water, plant life. It could be perfect."

"I'm with Abigail," said Finn. "This could be the type of planet we've been looking for. Besides, it has two suns. That's kind of cool."

"Well, I'm with Elias," said Vale. "Unless he's planning to set more things on fire. Then I am definitely *not* with Elias."

"I want to go with you!" said Finn's little sister, Paige. She popped her head out from under the table, where she'd been hiding the whole time. "It doesn't sound boring to me!"

"Paige, you're too young," said Finn. "And too weird. Get out from under the table."

Paige crawled out just as Voltronix Zu walked into the hall.

"HELLO, YOUNG EXPLORERS. I AM AWESOME," said the robot.

The kids all stared up at Voltronix.

"Can we help you with something?" said Abigail.

"YOU HELP ME? THAT IS HILARIOUS. BUT ALSO YES," said Voltronix. "CAPTAIN CASPIAN HAS GIVEN ME THIS DOOHICKEY AND TOLD ME TO USE IT. WHAT IS IT?"

Voltronix held up a thin metal tube about the size of a large baseball bat.

"It looks like an old-timey telescope," said Vale. "Or like a pirate's spyglass. You know, that thing they would hold up to their eyes to see ships sailing in the distance."

"THAT'S NOT IT," said Voltronix. "SAY SOMETHING ELSE. BUT MAKE IT RIGHT THIS TIME."

"Wow, you're rude," said Finn. "Elias, could you take a look at it? I bet you could figure it out."

Finn hoped that Elias would get excited to test out a new technology. But Elias just sighed and took the tube from Voltronix.

"It's an investigative scope," said Elias, handing it back to Voltronix.

"Wow, Elias," said Finn. "How did you figure that out so fast?"

"It says the name right on the side," said Elias. Voltronix started to say something, but Elias stopped him. "And before you ask, I don't know what that means."

"It's our other new invention," said Finn's mom. She walked back to their table carrying a tray of food. "It lets you look through the surface of objects so you can see what's inside them. It's like if you took an X-ray and a telescope and mashed them together."

"That's so cool," said Vale. He stood up and took the scope from Voltronix Zu. He raised it to his eye and pointed it at Finn's head. "Just as I suspected. Empty."

"Get out of here," said Finn. He grabbed the scope and pointed it at the floor. "Whoa, cool! I can see the library below us. Through the floor!"

"Can I see?" asked Paige, dancing around her brother.

"Give me a second," said Finn.

"One Mississippi," said Page. "My turn."

Finn ignored his sister.

"A thousand and one Mississippis, come on, Finn, let me see!" Paige climbed her brother, trying to get at the scope.

"I'm glad you all like it," said Captain Caspian. She took it from Finn's hand and gave it to Paige. "Because you're taking it with you on your mission. We think we know what's on the surface of the planet. But we want to know what's underneath."

The kids all smiled. Suddenly, their visit to the boring, lifeless planet below them became a little more exciting.

"That's why I gave it to Voltronix Zu," said Captain Caspian. She took the scope from Paige, who was waggling it at Finn. "He'll be using it to record data about the planet."

"Wait a second, Mom," said Finn. "Are you telling me that . . . ?"

He couldn't bring himself to say it.

"Yes," said Captain Caspian. "Voltronix is going with you."

"YOU ARE GOING WITH ME. AREN'T YOU LUCKY?" said Voltronix.

"Can I go, too?" asked Paige.

"No!" said everybody. Everybody except Voltronix, who was polishing his metal arm so he could see his own reflection.

"I LOOK GOOD," he said.

Suddenly, the kids were less excited about their mission.

Chapter Five
Suitable Suits

Finn secured Elias's helmet. Abigail made sure Vale's gloves were fully attached to the rest of his space suit. Foggy checked Finn's boots. It took a surprising amount of teamwork to put on all their gear. Finn fastened Elias's helmet and knocked three times.

"Earth to Elias!" said Finn.

"That's not annoying," said Elias.

"What's up with you?" asked Finn. "Are you still thinking about your robot?"

"Sorta," said Elias.

"You're sorta thinking, or you are thinking but it's sorta about the robot?" asked Vale. "I'm lost."

Elias shook his head.

"It was supposed to be a surprise," said Elias. "I thought I could build us something that would really help us down on a planet. I know I'm not that much help out there, but at least I could be helpful up here."

"Not helpful?" said Abigail. "What are you talking about, Elias? You're part of the team."

"It's fine," said Elias. "I don't really want to talk about it. Anyway, the robot was supposed to be a surprise. The first robot to have its own intelligence. Turns out my parents beat me to it with Voltronix."

"I beg your pardon," said Foggy. When Finn had turned eight years old, his parents had given him Foggy. Finn had downloaded *Around the World in Eighty Days* by Jules Verne onto Foggy's mainframe. Ever since, Foggy had always been up for adventure. "I like to think that I have my own intelligence."

"No, that's not what I mean," said Elias. "I mean intelligence as a computing term. It means the way a computer thinks, not how smart it is."

"DID SOMEBODY SAY INTELLI-GENT?!" Voltronix Zu came around the corner. The light sparkled off his chrome body. "WERE YOU TALKING ABOUT ME? BECAUSE I AM THAT. THAT WORD YOU JUST SAID. I FORGET WHAT IT WAS."

Foggy sighed.

"This guy, again," he muttered.

Captain Caspian and Paige walked up behind Voltronix.

"Explorers Troop 301!" said Finn's mother. "We are all excited for you to investigate this very unusual planet."

"Can't wait!" said Paige. She pulled a space suit off a hook on the wall.

"You're not coming," said Finn.

"It's going to be so fun," said Paige, ignoring her brother.

"Mom?" said Finn.

"Who's going to help me put on my helmet?" asked Paige as she slipped one arm into a sleeve of the space suit.

"Someday soon," Captain Caspian said to Paige. She reached down and pulled her daughter out of the space suit. But Paige still clung to it like a life raft.

"For now, this planet is for Explorers Troop 301. And as you know, this could be a major find. It seems practically perfect. And yet, we see no signs of intelligent life."

"Speaking of which," said Finn. He pulled his mother to the side. "Mom, do we really need Voltronix to come with us? He seems a little . . . off."

"OFF?" said Voltronix. "NO WAY. SEE THIS GREEN LIGHT RIGHT HERE?" Voltronix pointed to his left shoulder. There was no green light.

"Wrong shoulder," muttered Foggy.

"RIGHT!" said Voltronix. He pointed to

his right shoulder. "THAT GREEN LIGHT MEANS I AM ON. VERY NOT OFF."

"That's right, Voltronix," said Captain Caspian. She was talking to the robot like he was a little kid. She turned to Finn and frowned. "Be nice, Finn. Voltronix is still working out the kinks. That's why I think it would be great if you let him be a part of your team. Elias, you can be in charge of helping Voltronix learn."

Elias was busy putting his space helmet back together. He had taken it off and pulled it apart to see how the visor worked, but was having trouble getting it to seal right.

"Me? Why me?" asked Elias.

"You're chief technologist," said Captain Caspian. "Who better?"

"Literally anybody," said Elias. "He smashed my robot!"

"Come on, Elias," Finn whispered. "How bad can it be? Maybe you can figure out where your robot went wrong."

"Hmm, maybe you're right," said Elias. "First I need to figure out this visor. Can we hold the mission for fifteen minutes while I fix this?"

"ABSOLUTELY NOT. ADVENTURE AWAITS, AND VOLTRONIX ZU NEVER AWAITS!" said the robot.

Elias looked up at Voltronix. The tall robot was looking right at him through the investigative scope.

"YOU HAVE A VERY NICE SPLEEN. I CAN SEE YOUR SPLEEN," said Voltronix.

"Hey," said Elias. "That's *my* spleen. Get your own."

Chapter Six
The Deafening Silence

Even as they stepped out of the explorer pod and onto the surface of the planet, the explorers knew something was going to go wrong. Abigail had landed their pod in what looked like a meadow. Tall yellow grass bent and swayed as the pod settled down. The hatch opened, and the explorers noticed it at once.

The silence.

Nothing made a sound. The friends stepped out onto the planet, and they heard their boots crunch on the grass. But other than that, there was nothing. No birds chirping, no wind rustling the leaves of the trees in the distance.

"This is weird," whispered Finn. "Try to stay as quiet as possible."

"I agree," whispered Vale. "If there is something on this planet, it will hear us from miles away with all this quiet."

"I DON'T KNOW WHY YOU'RE SO WORRIED. THIS IS FUN," shouted Voltronix. He stomped away from the explorer pod.

"Where are you going?!" Abigail asked. She tried to both whisper and yell at the same time.

"YOU SOUND WEIRD. I SOUND AWESOME," said Voltronix. "LET'S GO OVER THERE." Voltronix pointed at the river just beyond a small hill.

"Elias, get him under control," said Abigail. "It's your job!"

"I didn't ask for this," said Elias. "Foggy, can you help me out here?"

"Hey, he's the intelligent one," said Foggy. Voltronix tripped on a rock and fell flat on his face.

"WHO PUT A THING THERE?!" said the robot as he picked himself up. "NOT AWESOME!"

"Guys, at some point, we need to work with him as part of the team," said Finn. Voltronix started yelling at the rock he had tripped over. "Okay, maybe not right now, but at some point."

Elias sighed.

"Voltronix, that rock isn't alive. It can't hear you," he said.

"OH, IT CAN HEAR ME. IT'S JUST IGNORING ME!" shouted Voltronix.

At a rock. "AREN'T YOU?! AREN'T YOOOUUU???!!"

"You know," said Elias. "The best thing you can do to someone who's ignoring you? Ignore them back. It drives them crazy."

Voltronix nodded.

"YOU ARE WISE, LITTLE PERSON," said Voltronix. "I AM IGNORING YOU NOW, ROCK!"

Elias had successfully quieted Voltronix. He turned to share the moment with Finn, but no one was there to witness it. His friends had all kept going. Elias hustled to catch up.

The crew made their way across the field, over the hill, and to the body of water on the other side. They walked carefully and quietly. The only sounds they heard were their own boots on the ground and the swishing of their space-suit pant legs as they walked. Occasionally Voltronix would threaten a rock not to trip him. But other than that, total silence.

They slowly approached the water's edge. They all looked around for some sign of animal life. There were short trees nearby, but they couldn't see any birds. Vale checked what looked like tidal pools, but there was nothing but some dark blue moss. No frogs, no crabs. Nothing.

"This really does look like a planet where humans could live," Foggy said quietly. "My sensors say you could breathe the air."

"Let's keep our helmets on for now," said

Abigail. "Those are the rules. Besides, something feels off."

"I BET SOMETHING LIVES IN THE WATER, AND I BET I AM RIGHT," said Voltronix.

Finn picked up a small stone and tossed it into the water. It splashed and rippled across the surface. But nothing happened.

"Hey, I thought this was supposed to be a river," said Vale. "The water is so still. It's more like a lake."

"I BET SOMETHING LIVES IN THE WATER, AND I BET I AM RIGHT," said Voltronix.

"Then why don't you go for a swim and find out?" said Elias. "Let us know if a shark bites you."

"OKAY. HOW DO I SWIM?" asked Voltronix as he walked into the water.

"No, stop!" said Foggy. "It's not smart to

just go into water like that. You don't know what's in there."

"HA HA HA HA, I LAUGH," said Voltronix. "I AM VOLTRONIX ZU! I AM NOT AFRAID OF ANYTHING." The robot kept walking. The water rose to his chest. "I KNOW YOU ALL LAUGH AT ME. YOU THINK I DON'T KNOW, BUT I DO KNOW. I AM NOT AFRAID OF YOUR LAUGHTER, AND I AM NOT AFRAID OF THE WATER. I AM WATERPROOF!"

Voltronix was now in the water up to his chin.

"BUT COULD SOMEONE TELL ME HOW TO SWIM NOW?"

"For crying out loud," said Abigail. "Voltronix, you don't have to prove anything to us. Come back here, please."

The robot seemed relieved and began walking back to shore.

"Besides, I think it's time we started using this," said Elias. He held up the investigative scope. He peered down at the ground. "I don't see anything but a bunch of rock."

"HEY, THAT'S MINE. HOW DID YOU GET THAT?" asked Voltronix. He stepped out of the water, dripping, and reached for the scope.

"Here," said Elias. He handed Voltronix the scope. "I just didn't want it to get wet. Why don't you use it to see if there is anything alive in the water?"

"THAT IS A GOOD IDEA THAT I

THOUGHT OF FIRST BUT AM SAYING SECOND," said Voltronix. "I WILL USE THE DOOHICKEY TO SEE WHAT'S IN THE WATER."

Voltronix had rocket boosters in his feet, just like Foggy. He flew up over the water and hovered there. He held the scope up to his eye and peered down at the water.

"I DON'T SEE ANYTHING," said Voltronix.

"I knew it," said Vale. "What happened to 'I bet something lives in the water'?"

"I BET IT DOES. I JUST NEED TO TURN UP THE POWER ON THIS DOO-HICKEY," said Voltronix. He reached over and turned a dial on the scope's side. "I BET WITH A LITTLE MORE POWER I WILL SEE THAT SOMETHING LIVES IN THE WATER."

The explorers sat down on the grass at the water's edge.

"THERE. I'VE INCREASED THE POWER, AND NOW I CAN CLEARLY SEE THERE'S NOTHING THERE. I MEAN, MAYBE IT NEEDS MORE POWER."

"Come on, guys," said Abigail. "Let's explore some more. Voltronix, you too!"

"VOLTRONIX ZU IS NEVER WRONG," the robot yelled. He turned another dial on the scope. "JUST YOU WAIT. THERE IS SOMETHING DOWN THERE."

"Voltronix," said Elias. "What are you doing? Something's going wrong."

The scope in Voltronix's hands had started to glow red.

"I THINK I SEE SOMETHING," said the robot.

The river below Voltronix started to churn.

Waves began rising from the still water.

"Turn it off," said Abigail. "Turn it off, Voltronix. Please!"

"NO!" Voltronix looked at the explorers. "YOU ALL SAID I WAS WRONG, BUT I AM RIGHT. I, VOLTRONIX ZU, AM INTELLIGENT."

He reached down and twisted the scope. It glowed a bright purple.

"Foggy," said Finn. "Can you please go up there and take that away from him?"

The water rose even higher. It started to look like a tidal wave was rising toward Voltronix.

"It's going to crash over us!" shouted Vale. "Get back!"

The explorers scrambled away from the river just as Foggy reached Voltronix.

"UNHAND ME!" cried Voltronix. "I AM VOLTRONIX ZU."

"Sorry, chum," said Foggy. "But it looks like this scope is causing problems down below. Time to turn it off."

"OKAY, FINE!" said Voltronix.

He reached down and twisted one of the dials on the scope.

"No, you're supposed to turn it counterclockwise to turn it off," said Foggy.

"THIS IS COUNTERCLOCKWISE."

"No," said Foggy. "That's clockwise."

The scope glowed bright white. The waves beneath them surged. The ground rumbled.

"Voltronix, my friend!" yelled Foggy. "That's clockwise!"

"YOU'RE CLOCKWISE!" shouted Voltronix.

"What?" said Foggy.

And that's when the planet turned inside out. Sort of.

Chapter Seven
Vale Figures It Out

The investigative scope that Captain Caspian gave to Explorers Troop 301 was experimental. It had only been tested on everyday objects aboard the *Marlowe*. One engineer used it to see what the chefs had planned for dinner by looking through the fridge door. Another used it to find his favorite pen, which had rolled behind a couch. Everyone thought its power was limited. When Captain Caspian gave it to the explorers, she didn't think it was any more dangerous than their shoelaces.

In other words, it was something for them to play with while they were on a boring planet.

Where Captain Caspian went wrong was handing the experimental technology to Voltronix Zu. Voltronix Zu was also experimental technology. He was, if you think about it, a baby. A big, shiny metal baby who was really loud and thought he knew everything.

So when he saw Foggy flying at him, Voltronix wanted to prove himself. Who was this other robot to stop him? And who were those kids to boss him around? He was Voltronix Zu! The most important robot in the entire universe. He was made special.

He wasn't going to listen to anything anyone told him. And so he cranked the scope up as high as it would go. He held Foggy off and raised it to his eye.

"THERE! I CAN SEE IT!" shouted Voltronix. "THERE IS SOMETHING DOWN THERE. I TOLD YOU!" Voltronix pointed at Foggy. "AND I TOLD YOU AND YOU AND YOU AND YOU." Voltronix pointed at the kids as they ran back up the hill.

The river beneath Foggy and Voltronix began to open. The water rushed away from the middle. The grass the kids ran across began to disappear into the dirt. It was like some underground giant was grabbing the roots and pulling each blade down through the surface.

"This is bad, right?" said Vale.

"I DID IT!" yelled Voltronix Zu. "I, VOLTRONIX ZU, SOLVED THE MYSTERY OF THIS PLANET. I CAN SEE THEM NOW. THE LIFE-FORMS WHO LIVE HERE. THEY'RE CLIMBING UP."

"Yeah, that sounds bad," said Abigail. "I

doubt it's a welcoming committee."

"Foggy, Voltronix!" yelled Finn. "Please. Come here! We need to stick together."

The two robots flew to where the kids stood atop the hill. Their explorer pod was parked just a few hundred yards away. But they all stood still and watched as a mountain began rising from the river. The water flowed away and spread across the land.

"Oh no, Voltronix," said Abigail. "What did you do?"

"I MADE A MOUNTAIN," said Voltron-ix. "AMAZING! I, VOLTRONIX ZU, HAVE MADE A MOUNTAIN."

"I don't know if that's as cool as you think it is, Voltronix," said Abigail.

"WHAT?! IT'S SUPER COOL," said the robot. He was now literally patting himself on the back again. He was really good at that. "HOW LONG DOES IT TAKE A STUPID PLANET TO MAKE A MOUNTAIN? A BILLION YEARS?! I DID IT IN WAY LESS

THAN THAT. STUPID PLANET."

"I don't think that's a mountain," said Finn. "Look. There's no peak, and it's open at the top. I think you made a volcano, Voltronix!"

"OH, IS THAT COOL, TOO?!"

"No!" shouted all the explorers at once. They hugged each other and waited for an explosion.

But nothing came. No lava. No bursts of burning ash or clouds of smoke. It was like the rest of the planet. Silent.

"I can't believe you guys did that. Is this what you're like all the time?"

The explorers all spun around. The hatch of their explorer pod was open. And marching toward them, in a space suit way too big for her, was Paige.

"Paige?!" said Finn. "What are you doing here?!"

"I don't know what you guys did with that

scope thing, but the bubble aliens say you turned their planet inside out and ruined everything," said Paige, getting closer.

"What are bubble aliens?" said Foggy. "They sound cute."

"Paige!" shouted Finn. "What. Are. You. Doing. Here?!"

"If you had taken even a second to look around before you destroyed their planet, you would have seen them," said Paige. She was standing right in front of them now. And, to everyone's surprise, circling around her head were bubbles. Small bubbles. They looked like the kind of tiny bubbles you wipe off a bubble wand after you've blown your big bubbles.

"Are there miniature aliens inside the bubbles?" said Foggy. "This is getting so cute!"

"Paige!" yelled Finn. "WHAT ARE YOU DOING HERE?!"

"Oh, I borrowed your extra space suit and stowed away inside the storage cupboard in the explorer pod," she said. "It's a good thing I did, too. If I hadn't come, you guys wouldn't even know about the bubble aliens. They're called Fuffles."

"It just keeps getting cuter!" said Foggy.

"And the Fuffles are upset," said Paige. "Because you've turned the planet inside out!"

"Technically, the planet isn't inside out," said Elias. "If it was inside out, then the inner core of the planet would be outside and we would be trapped inside."

"Maybe it's like a sock," said Vale.

"What?!" said Elias. He was too stressed out to hear one of Vale's jokes.

"Like, you know how a sock gets turned inside out, but not all the way?" said Vale, excited by his theory. "Like if the toe of the sock gets pulled through, and you see the fuzzy inside of the toe but not the fuzzy inside of the rest of the sock. I would call that inside out. Wouldn't you?"

Elias shook his head.

"You see," said Vale, now acting like the smartest kid in the universe. "In my theory, the planet is the sock and the volcano is the fuzzy toe. Ladies and gentlemen, if I am correct—"

"The Fuffles!" shouted Paige, interrupting Vale. "Don't care! About your socks! They care about the rock giants now climbing up out of the inside of the planet!"

"HA HA HA, THAT'S HILARIOUS. THERE ARE NO ROCK GIANTS," said Voltronix.

CLANG.

A rock bounced off Voltronix's head.

The crew all turned toward volcano. A giant that looked like it was made of ten boulders all held together by ten other boulders stood at the top. It picked up a rock off the ground.

"OKAY, SO ONE ROCK GIANT," said Voltronix. "THAT'S HARDLY—"

CLANG.

Another rock bounced off Voltronix's head. Another rock giant had climbed out of the volcano.

"OKAY, SO TWO ROCK GIANTS," said Voltronix.

Five more rock giants climbed out of the volcano.

"OKAY, LET'S GO HOME!" said Voltronix.

Chapter Eight
The Fuffles Speak

The explorers explained to Voltronix why they couldn't go home. Elias told him that it was right there in the explorer handbook. Never leave a planet worse off than it was before you found it.

"IT'S NOT WORSE!" said Voltronix. He began to walk back to the pod. "WHO DOESN'T LIKE VOLCANOES? ANYWAY,

JOB WELL DONE, ME. LET'S GO HOME."

"Voltronix, stay," said Elias. Voltronix stopped and turned around. "Good robot."

The bubbles floating in the air started to zip around Paige's head. She laughed.

"No, we're not going to leave you like this," she told the Fuffles. "We'll fix it. My brother won't let anything happen to you, right, Finn?"

Finn was busy trying to figure out how he was going to explain to his mother that they'd turned this easy, boring planet into a war zone. And how he was going to explain that his little sister had come with them into the war zone. And what a Fuffle was. That actually seemed to be the easiest problem to solve.

"Right, I guess," said Finn. "First things first. Fuffles. What are you?"

New bubbles popped into view around Finn's head. They began spinning in circles, like a mini tornado had touched down around Finn's helmet. The air around his head began buzzing, and then the buzzing grew faster and faster.

Soon, in the high-pitched drone of the bubble tornado, he could hear words. It was like a silly joke Vale liked to play on the *Marlowe*. He'd stand behind one of the station's large fans and speak through it. His voice would come through all chopped up and funny-sounding.

The Fuffles sounded like this:

"zzzzzzzzzzzzzzzWEzzzzzzzzAREzzzz zzAzzzzzzzzPEACEFULzzzzzzzzzzzzzzzzz CIVILIZATIONzzzzzzzzzzzzzzzzzzzzzzzzzz FORzzzzzzzzzYEARSzzzzzzzWEzzzzzzzz WEREzzzTHREATENEDzzzBYzzzzzzzzzzz THEzzzzzROCKzzzzzzzzzzzGIANTSzzzz zzzzzzzzzzzWHOzzzzzzzzzzzzCRAWLED zzzzzzzzzOUTzzzzzzzzzzzzzOFzzzzzzzzz THEzzzzzzGROUNDzzzzzzzzzANDzzzzz zzzzzzNEARLYzzzzzDESTROYEDzzzzzzz THE PLANET."

"That's terrible," said Finn. He held up his hand to the rest of the troop, who wondered what the Fuffles were saying. "We had a situation like that on our last planet, where two different species couldn't get along."

"*THATzzzzzzzzISzzzzzzNOTzzzzzzzzz OURzzzzzzPROBLEM.*"

The Fuffles explained to Finn that the rock giants were not evil. They didn't mean to do the Fuffles harm. But they were so big, they couldn't help but pop the Fuffles' bubbles when they walked or swung their arms. Often, just their bellowing voices would be too much for the fragile bubbles.

"And what happens when one of your bubbles bursts?" said Finn. "Can you make a new one?"

"*WEzzzzzzAREzzzzzzzTHEzzzzzzzzzz BUBBLES,*" said the aliens spinning around Finn's head. "*THEzzzzzzzBUBBLESzzzzzzzz AREzzzzzzUSzzzzzCANzzzzzYOUzzzzzzz MAKEzzzzzzzzAzzzzzzzzNEWzzzzzzzzzz*

ONEzzzzzzzzOFzzzzzzzzzYOUzzzzzzzzzz
IFzzzzzzYOUzzzzzzAREzzzzzz POPPED?"

"I don't think so," said Finn. "And I don't want to find out." He explained to his friends what the aliens had told him.

"THAT'S WEIRD," said Voltronix. "I UNDERSTAND IT PERFECTLY, BUT WHY DON'T YOU EXPLAIN IT A LIT-TLE BETTER TO EVERYONE ELSE."

"So those giant rock guys coming out of that volcano and walking toward us, they're not evil?" said Vale. "Because they look pretty evil."

"I think they're not smart enough to be evil," said Finn. "But that doesn't mean they can't do a lot of damage. They move by instinct. They don't think. They just do what their bodies tell them to do. Think of them as big rock bugs."

"That doesn't make me feel better," said Vale. "Look out!" One of the giants threw a boulder at the troop. They all scattered before it landed like a meteor a few yards away.

"Well, at least their aim isn't very good," said Vale.

Another boulder came crashing down, this time right next to the explorer pod.

"Okay, it's pretty good," said Vale. "We better run."

Chapter Nine
My Kingdom for a Plan

"We are not splitting up again," said Abigail as the troop tried to figure out what to do next. "You remember what happened when we split up on that other planet? It ended up breaking in two! We're a team, and we need to stay as a team. Come on, this way."

The troop followed Abigail as she ran

toward a patch of tall grass, away from the river but also far from their almost-crushed explorer pod. They knelt low in the grass so the giants couldn't see them.

"We need a plan," said Abigail. "Finn, what do you have?"

"Does 'stay here and hope the giants don't find us' count as a plan?" said Finn. A boulder crashed down about twenty feet from where they huddled. "Guess not."

"How do they know where we are?" asked Elias. "I wonder if they have some sort of sixth sense that lets them see without seeing, you know?"

"Nope," said Vale. "It's Voltronix."

While the troop and Foggy had all been kneeling in the grass, Voltronix was standing behind them, watching the rock giants.

"WHO DO YOU THINK IS TALLER,

THEM OR ME?" asked Voltronix. "ME, RIGHT? I KNOW THEY'RE CALLED GIANTS BUT—"

"Will you get down here?" said Elias. He pulled on the robot's arm until Voltronix ducked behind the grass.

The group crawled a little farther away.

"The Fuffles said the giants are actually from underground," said Abigail. "Maybe if we can get underground, we can talk to them and convince them to stay there."

"I don't know," said Paige. "The Fuffles said the rock giants don't really have brains. I don't know if there's a way to talk to them."

"Paige, be quiet! You're not even supposed to be here!" said Finn. Abigail gave Finn a dirty look.

"But you're also right," said Finn. He gritted his teeth. "So I'm sorry. I don't think there's any reasoning with the giants."

"What about the volcano?" asked Elias. "Maybe if we can somehow lure them back there, we could reverse the volcano and send them back where they came from?"

A series of bubbles popped up around Elias's head and started spinning.

"Whoa, this is weird," said Elias. "Okay, the Fuffles say they think the giants came up because they are drawn to the light. It's complete darkness underground."

"So all we have to do is wait till nighttime and they'll stop?" said Vale. "I can do that."

"Two suns," said Elias. "No nighttime."

ROOOAAARRRRRRRR.

The giants stomping down the volcano bellowed. It was the loudest sound the explorers had ever heard. Several of the bubbles around their heads began to shake, as if they were going to pop.

"Oh no," said Paige. "The Fuffles!"

Chapter Ten
Paige to the Rescue

More bubble aliens appeared around the explorers' heads. Each kid now had a bubble tornado spinning around their helmet. The Fuffles were upset. They were scared. And they wanted the explorers to fix this mess before anyone popped.

But Finn and his friends weren't sure what to do. A few of the giants had reached the base of the volcano and were making their way toward the explorer pod. Another boulder crashed a few yards away from where they huddled.

"The Fuffles may think these giants don't mean any harm," said Vale, "but it looks like they mean to harm *us*!"

The explorers stayed low and crawled farther from the giants. There had to be a dozen of the rock monsters now stomping down the mountain and out into the grass.

"I have an idea," said Paige.

"Not now," said Finn.

"But I think if I take off my helmet—" said Paige.

"Are you nuts?" said Finn. "We don't know if we can breathe this air. It could be really poisonous."

"But wait," said Paige.

"Nope," said Finn. "The fact is, you have no idea what could happen if you expose yourself to the air of an alien planet. Even if Mom thinks it's a lot like Earth's. It's all in the explorer handbook, which you would have read if you were an actual explorer!"

Paige looked like she might cry.

"May I make a suggestion?" asked Foggy as they crawled through the tall grass. "The rock giants all seem to be curious about our explorer pod. Could we circle around and check out the volcano while they're distracted? Then we'll see if there's anything we can do."

The bubbles spun around their heads, warning the explorers that heading toward the volcano was dangerous.

"Let's do it," said Abigail. "But stay low and keep close."

Carefully and quietly, the explorers waded through the shallow water, crossing the river and approaching the volcano.

"Now I know why the Fuffles stay so quiet," said Vale. "So they don't attract the attention of the giants."

The explorers tiptoed to the base of the volcano. It was covered in loose rocks and dust, all kicked up from underground. Finn bent down and grabbed a rock. "Huh, it's cold," he said. "The core of this planet must be ice. If it was magma like the last planet, this rock would still be hot."

"BORING!" said Voltronix Zu. "WE

HAVEN'T TALKED ABOUT ME IN A WHILE. WHAT SHOULD I DO?"

Everyone shushed him.

"Nothing," whispered Elias. "Pretend we're in a competition to see who can be quietest."

"OH, I CAN BE SUPER QUIET," said Voltronix. "YOU DON'T EVEN KNOW HOW QUIET I CAN BE. I CAN BE QUIET LIKE A MOUSE. AND I DON'T MEAN THE ANIMAL MOUSE. I MEAN LIKE A COMPUTER MOUSE SITTING ON A DESK DOING NOTHING. THAT'S HOW QUIET I CAN BE. SO HA!"

ROARRRRRRRR.

The explorers had been spotted. The rock giants, seeing the kids near the volcano, seemed to be furious. And their collective yell shook even more Fuffles.

"We need to save the Fuffles," said Paige. "One more yell from those giants could pop the bubbles."

"But what are we supposed to do?" said Finn. "We can't just shush them."

"We have to *protect* them," said Paige. "There's only one way. Fuffles, on my count."

"Paige, what are you doing?" asked Finn.

"One," said Paige.

"What are you counting down, Paige?" said Finn.

"Two," said Paige.

"Finn, whatever she's doing, tell her to stop," said Abigail.

"You've known her for her whole life," said Finn. "Has she ever listened to me? Paige, stop."

"Three," said Paige. She took a big gulp of air and puffed out her cheeks, then shut her eyes.

"Oh no," said Finn. "I said don't!"

Paige reached up and pressed a button on the side of her helmet.

"No!" shouted Finn.

The glass visor on her helmet lifted, exposing Paige's head to the elements of the strange planet.

Chapter Eleven
A Handbook Never Lies

Never take off your helmet on an unfamiliar planet.
It says so right in the explorer handbook.
Finn had read the section a hundred times. So
many things could go wrong if someone tried
to breathe alien air. They could choke. They
could be poisoned. They could turn purple.
They could turn orange. They could turn
hairy. They could turn scaly. They could grow

gills. They could turn into a cloud. They could turn into a puddle. They could turn into a frog. They could turn into a tadpole, which is a baby frog, which is weird.

"Paige!" cried Finn. He was so scared for his sister. But before he could do anything, the Fuffles around everyone's heads zipped into her space suit.

Finn dove at Paige and slapped the button on the side of her helmet before she could take a breath. Her visor shut. Finn could barely see his sister's face. It was like she was under a bubbling ocean.

"Paige!" yelled Finn. The giants bellowed at his cry, but he didn't care. "Paige! Can you hear me?"

Paige opened her eyes. And Finn could just see through all the bubbles that she was smiling.

"I'm fine, Finn," she said. "You worry too much."

Paige turned to the other explorers.

"Is he always like this on your adventures?"

"ALWAYS," said Voltronix.

"First of all, you've never been on an exploration," Finn said to Voltronix. "And second of all. PAIGE! You're not supposed to be on this one, and you're not supposed to open your visor like that. You could have been poisoned!

Or turned into a tadpole!"

"I had to do something," said Paige. "And look, it worked."

Paige was right. Even though the giants had roared, none of the Fuffles had popped. The glass of her helmet had absorbed the vibrations. The tiny aliens were safe.

Click.

"Sorry," said Foggy. "I just had to take a picture of this with my eye camera. Cute little Paige with all those cute little Fuffles. It's too much!"

ROOOARRRRR.

The giants were getting closer. Luckily, it seemed no more were coming out of the volcano. For now.

"This is a tricky situation," said Abigail. "It's not like the rock giants are bad, right? They just don't belong here. And they don't know they don't belong here."

"Yeah, that's it!" said Elias. "They're like an invasive species. You know, like we were talking about in science class! It's when a plant or an animal is brought to a different place. And that plant may not belong there, but it starts growing. And then it takes over the plants that were born there. The plant isn't evil. It's not the plant's fault it was brought into a new environment."

Elias smiled at his friends. None of them smiled back.

"Elias is totally right," Finn said. "They're like an invasive species."

"Great," said Vale. "But Elias said, 'That's it,' in the middle of us being chased by giant rock monsters. You really should mean 'That's it, I have a plan to get us out of this.' Not 'That's it, this is like that one science homework.'"

"Oh," said Elias. "I guess that's true. Well, the good news is that the rock monsters aren't technically chasing us yet."

"Then, Elias, friend, I have bad news for you," said Foggy. "Because here they come." The explorers all turned and saw that about six of the rock monsters had turned around, abandoned the explorer pod, and were now running straight at them.

Chapter Twelve
Gold-Medal Vale

You really never know how fast you can run until you have rock giants taking huge strides right toward you. It turns out, kids can run pretty fast. But not fast enough. The giants were easily gaining on them.

"Foggy!" yelled Abigail. "Voltronix! You know what to do!"

"NOPE!" said Voltronix. "I DON'T

KNOW WHAT TO DO." Foggy turned on his rocket boosters and swept Paige, Finn, and Vale up in his arms. Voltronix turned around.

"OH, I'M SUPPOSED TO DO THAT," said Voltronix "OKAY!"

Voltronix grabbed Abigail and Elias and flew up into the air. The rock giants bellowed again and ran even faster at the flying kids.

"Paige!" yelled Finn. "Are the Fuffles saying anything? Do they have any advice for how to get out of here?!"

"Not really!" said Paige. "They're mostly just screaming, '*zzzzzzzAAHHHHHHHzzzzzzz AAAAHHHHHHHzzzzzzzzzAHHHHHHH-HHH!*'"

"Great," said Finn.

"Okay, this is it," said Vale. "My turn."

"Your turn?" said Finn. "What do you mean?"

"Well, Abigail makes decisions, you solve problems, and Elias fixes stuff," said Vale. "So you three do that. You: figure out the problem. Elias: engineer something. Abigail: lead the way."

"And what are you going to do?" asked Finn.

"I'm going to do my patented move."

Vale raised his arms and slipped out of Foggy's grasp, tumbling to the ground. He somersaulted and stood up.

"Get to the top of the volcano!" he yelled. "See if there's something you can do! I'll distract the rock dummies!"

Vale jumped up and down, clapping his hands until the rock giants noticed that he'd dropped to the ground. They turned immediately and began chasing him.

"Whoops!" Vale said, running away from the volcano and back toward the grass.

"What is he going to do?" asked Abigail.

"I don't know," said Finn. "He's been practicing all these new acrobatic moves. I guess he thinks he's going to do those. But really, he's probably going to get smooshed."

"Should we stop him?" said Abigail.

"Do you know any acrobatics?" asked Finn.

Foggy took off toward the top of the volcano and Voltronix followed.

"I'M FASTER!" yelled Voltronix, trailing behind Foggy.

Finn looked back and watched as Vale jumped and rolled, dodging all the rocks the giants threw his way.

But soon, six of the giants had Vale surrounded. Vale didn't seem worried. He danced around the middle of the circle of giants. He was enjoying himself.

"Oh no, he's going to try it," said Finn.

"Try what?" said Paige.

"The triple-double-dutch-flip-somersault-jump-sidekick-with-a-smile," said Finn. "His new favorite move."

One of the giants leapt forward to grab Vale. But Vale sidestepped, jumped, and then bounced again on both feet.

"That's the triple," said Finn.

Another giant reached for Vale, but he leapt into the air and flipped backward. The giant missed and crashed into the first one.

"That's the double-dutch-flip," said Finn.

He was getting excited.

Two angry giants lunged at Vale, but he rolled beneath them and they crashed into each other.

"The somersault!" said Finn. "And the—"

Vale leapt out of the reach of the fifth giant, who piled onto the other four.

"The jump—" yelled Finn. He couldn't believe it!

The sixth and final giant was confused. It couldn't see Vale over the pile of its friends, and Vale kicked out, tripping the giant, who fell on top of the others.

"The sidekick!" cried Finn. "Unbelievable! And, wait for it!"

Vale waved to his friends, running toward the volcano. He was grinning from ear to ear.

"With a smile," said Finn. "I didn't think he could pull it off. But he did. Quick, let's get to the top!"

But there were six more giants running right behind the others. One of them reached down and grabbed Vale, lifting him off the ground.

"Oh no," said Finn. "That victory was short-lived."

Chapter Thirteen
Volcanoes All Around!

"They have Vale!" Finn shouted. But he could see from his friends' faces that they already knew. If they didn't do something fast, Vale would be rock-giant lunch.

Paige, Finn, and Foggy landed at the top of the volcano.

"We have to get back down there and get him," said Finn.

Voltronix landed just behind them, setting down Elias and Abigail.

"I WILL FIX THIS!" said Voltronix Zu.

"No!" yelled everyone.

"OH, I DON'T MIND," said Voltronix. "BUT THANKS. LET'S SEE."

Voltronix raised the scope again and began fiddling with the dials on the side.

"What are you doing?" said Elias.

"I'M GOING TO REVERSE WHAT FOGGY DID LAST TIME AND SEND THIS VOLCANO BACK DOWN INTO THE GROUND."

"Me?" said Foggy. "I told you counter-clockwise!"

"PRETTY SURE YOU SAID COUN-TERWISE, WHICH ISN'T EVEN A THING," said Voltronix. "I FORGIVE YOU. ANYWAY, LET ME SEE HERE. AHA. HERE WE GO. PROBLEM! MEET YOUR SOLUTION!"

The scope again lit up different colors, eventually turning white.

"Oh no, Voltronix," said Elias. "Not again."

Another volcano, just a football field away, started to spring up from the ground.

"HUH," said Voltronix. "FOGGY MUST HAVE BEEN WRONG ABOUT THAT ONE, TOO."

"Me?!" shouted Foggy. "I didn't do anything, chum!"

"Foggy, we need to get down there and save Vale," said Finn. "Voltronix is not going to do it."

"I BEG YOUR PARDON!" said Voltronix. He was surprised no one was telling him how awesome he was. "LOOK. PRESTO! EVERYTHING IS FIXED!"

Another volcano erupted from the ground. The rumbling nearly knocked the explorers over.

"Elias, can you take a look at the scope?" asked Abigail. "We need to get down there to Vale. I think they're squeezing him like a teddy bear."

"Me?" said Elias. "But don't you want someone else? It always takes me forever to do anything."

"Can't get any worse than Voltronix," said Finn.

"I don't know," said Elias. "The last thing I

built blew up in my room."

"Elias, you can do this," said Finn.

"And I never did make the breadshield," said Elias. "You know, I think if I could somehow get the scanner to tell a Danish from a doughnut, then—"

"ELIAS!" yelled Finn. "Stop talking about pastries. We believe in you. You are our chief technologist. You got this. We are all depending on you."

Finn, Abigail, and Foggy flew back down to the giants.

Foggy soared right at the rock monsters.

"This is fuunnnnnn!" he yelled as he circled the giant holding on to Vale. The giant swung a large hand at the robot, barely missing him.

"Okay, all depending on me," said Elias. "No big deal. Actually, big deal. Very big deal. Kind of a bigger deal than a breadshield."

Elias was starting to sweat.

"LET ME TRY ONE MORE TIME!" said Voltronix. He twisted more dials on the scope. Six small volcanoes shot up out of the volcano they were standing on.

"Oh, for Pete's sake!" said Paige. She grabbed the scope from Voltronix and handed it to Elias. "Just fix it already. Otherwise, we're done for."

Elias held up the scope. Giants were now crawling out of every volcano on the surface of the planet. He had to do something.

But what?

Chapter Fourteen
Homework Pays Off

Elias twisted and turned all the knobs and dials on the scope. He was better at it than Voltronix. He didn't accidentally make any volcanoes appear, but nothing he did reversed the damage the scope had done.

"Come on, Elias," said Paige. "Hurry."

"There's something wrong with this thing," said Elias.

"Ya think?" said Paige.

"No, I mean, it's supposed to just be a viewing device," said Elias. "You're only supposed to be able to *see* through it."

"That's great," said Paige. "By the way, a rock giant just caught Finn."

"There must be something else in the scope for it to be able to change a planet like this," said Elias.

"And now he has Abigail," said Paige. "Oh, and Foggy."

"Some kind of power source inside of it," said Elias.

"And now he's juggling with them," said Paige. "Elias? Can we move this along?"

"I don't know," said Elias. "Maybe, if I had like an hour to figure it out."

"The giant is now spinning Finn like a basketball on his finger," said Paige. "So, you probably have a little less time."

Elias wanted to be the hero. He wanted to be the one who saved the day. But this was just like when they were playing laser tag. Maybe he wasn't built for exploring. Maybe he should be back in a lab on the *Marlowe* taking things apart.

More rock giants crawled out of the volcanoes. They started to circle Paige, Elias, and Voltronix.

"HI, I'M VOLTRONIX ZU. I'M AWESOME. THANKS FOR ASKING," said Voltronix.

The giants bellowed back.

"Elias!" yelled Paige. He looked over at her with all the bubble aliens inside her helmet. He wished he could be as brave as she was. She'd risked her life to save the Fuffles. But he was much more comfortable with his notebook than with battling aliens. Everything was going to go up in flames, and it was his fault.

"Wait, that's it," said Elias. "Flames! Remember when I said the rock giants were an invasive species? Well, how do you get rid of an invasive species of plant? A controlled burn. You have to burn away the plant."

"Okay," said Paige. "But you can't burn rock."

"No, I guess not," said Elias. "And they're not evil, so we don't want to hurt them. But! Aha. Maybe we could use the flames a different way."

Elias twisted knobs and dials on the scope. And then, with one final flourish, he flipped a switch on the contraption and the whole thing lit up. It looked like it was on fire, but Elias could still hold it. It wasn't hot. Bright green, red, white, and purple lights shone out of it. The rock giants were transfixed. They couldn't take their eyes off of it. The giants on the ground put down the explorers and began climbing the volcano. They were attracted to the brilliant light of the scope.

"Great work, Elias! They're like giant, scary, strong rocky moths!" said Paige. "Except now they're all coming at us."

"VOLTRONIX ZU UNDERSTANDS!" said the robot.

"Yes, you do," said Elias. "You get it, you big bucket of bolts, don't you?"

"OF COURSE," said Voltronix. "YOU BROKE THE SCOPE, ELIAS! I WILL NOW THROW IT AWAY."

The robot picked up the scope and flew it into the sky. The giants all watched him as he spun, turned, and flew into the mouth of the volcano. Suddenly, the light from the scope came pouring out of all the holes in the ground. Red, green, blue, and purple light shot out of the mouths of the volcanoes. The giants were mesmerized,

and they all began following the light, climbing back down into the underground.

Foggy landed next to Elias and Paige. He placed Finn, Vale, and Abigail down on the ground.

"That was amazing, Elias," said Finn. "How did you do it?"

"Well, the first step to becoming a great engineer isn't to fix things," said Elias. "It's to break things. Then you can see how they work. And I'm really good at breaking things."

Voltronix Zu flew out of the mouth of the volcano and landed next to his friends.

"Voltronix!" said Abigail. "That was really smart and brave, putting that scope underground so the giants would be drawn to it and leave everyone up here alone."

"IS THAT WHAT I DID? YES, THAT IS WHAT I DID," said Voltronix. "YOU ARE WELCOME."

Chapter Fifteen
What Big Brothers Are For

The explorers happily flew their explorer pod back toward the *Famous Marlowe 280 Interplanetary Exploratory Space Station*. The tiny ship was cramped. Paige now sat on Finn's lap, rather than hiding in the storage compartment. And Voltronix kept standing up and swinging his arms around to relive how he'd saved the day.

When they docked their pod, Captain

Caspian was there waiting for them. She barely saw Finn. She grabbed Paige around the waist and gave her a big hug. It was a strange sight. Finn's mother was hugging and kissing the top of Paige's space helmet while also yelling at her for stowing away on the ship.

"KISS ME INSTEAD!" said Voltronix. "I SAVED THE PLANET. IN FACT, EVERYONE KISS ME!"

Finn slunk away with Abigail. He didn't think he'd done anything wrong. But he also knew that sometimes when a parent is mad at one child, it's easy for them to yell at the other kid, too.

"Hey, Finn, Abigail," said Elias. He ran to catch up to his friends. "I just wanted to say thanks."

"For what?" said Finn. "You're the one who

figured out how to stop the giants."

"And it was your terrible job of trying to fix the scope that made it burst into flames," laughed Abigail.

"Yeah," said Elias, laughing. "But I would never have been able to completely destroy that expensive equipment if you guys hadn't believed in me."

Elias hugged Finn. Abigail hugged Elias.

"Hey! No group hugs without me!" yelled Vale. "Triple-somersault-wingflap-hugathon!"

Vale crashed into his friends, and they all toppled over.

"Finn!" said Paige, walking up to the pile of explorers on the floor. "Mom wants to talk to you. And she is *mad*."

"At me?" said Finn.

"Yup."

"What did I do?"

"Oh," said Paige. "I may have told her that

I tried to get back in the pod and fly home but you wouldn't let me."

"FINN EMERSON CASPIAN!" yelled his mother. Finn looked at his sister. He was furious.

"Thanks for taking the heat for me on this one," said Paige. "What are big brothers for?"

Finn sighed. He knew he'd been outsmarted by Paige yet again.

"You know, you were pretty brave down there today," said Finn.

"FINN! EMERSON! CASPIAN!" shouted his mother again.

Finn sighed.

"Okay, I'll take the heat this one time, but only because you were so brave."

Finn looked over at Elias.

"You guys were both awesome," he said. "I know, Paige, you're still young, and, Elias, you were doubting yourself. But we needed you down there. You guys were—"

"FINN! EMERSON! CASPIAN! YOU BETTER GET OVER HERE RIGHT NOW!" yelled Captain Caspian.

"It's okay," said Paige. "I can finish that sentence for you. We were the best."

Finn laughed and slowly skulked back to where his mother was waiting.

Paige turned to Elias.

"Can I tell you something?" she asked. "My visor is stuck. I can't open it."

"Oh," said Elias. "I broke mine earlier, so I know how to fix it."

He reached over and pulled a panel off the side of her helmet. He twisted something inside, and the visor popped off. And, to everyone's surprise, one tiny bubble alien floated up to the ceiling.

"OOOOHH, BUBBLES," said Voltronix Zu. "I LOVE BUBBLES."

THE *FAMOUS MARLOWE 280 INTERPLANETARY EXPLORATORY SPACE STATION* HALL OF ROBOTS

FOR YEARS, THE ROBOTS OF THE *MARLOWE* HAVE BEEN UNIQUE IN THE UNIVERSE.

WHEN A CHILD ABOARD THE *MARLOWE* TURNS EIGHT, THEY ARE GIVEN THEIR OWN ROBOT. AND THAT CHILD GIVES THEIR ROBOT THEIR FAVORITE BOOK. THE ROBOT THEN TAKES ON THE PERSONALITY OF THAT BOOK.

EACH ROBOT IS MEMORIALIZED IN THIS, THE GREAT HALL OF ROBOTS.

Protofessor

The Original. Protofessor is the first robot to be given a book. The technology wasn't quite working yet, so he downloaded an entire library.

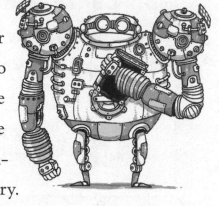

Now he is very confused. Much of what he says is gibberish. But every once in a while, he says something wise.

Hookbot

The Mistake. Hookbot was given *Peter Pan* by J. M. Barrie but took on the personality of the villain, Captain Hook, instead of the hero. Hookbot is convinced he is a feared space pirate. Rumor has it, he plunders galaxies far and wide.

Sir Lance-a-bot

The Legend. Young Genevieve Brooks gave her robot T. H. White's *The Once and Future King*. You may know the story as *The Sword in the Stone*. Sir Lance-a-bot is a mighty warrior, and he and Genevieve are legends aboard the *Marlowe*.

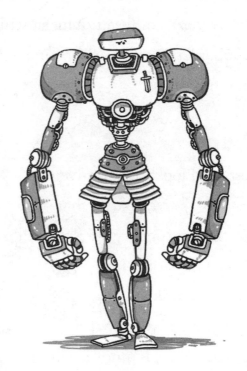

Foggy

The Question Mark. Finn Caspian didn't know what book to choose on his eighth birthday. And because he had avoided doing his homework, he ended up just grabbing *Around the World in Eighty Days* by Jules Verne. And so Foggy took on the personality of Phileas Fogg, which is why he can never quite sit still.

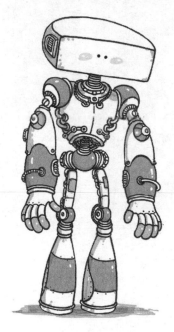

Blast off into more adventures, inspired by the award-winning kids' podcast!

HARPER
An Imprint of HarperCollinsPublishers

harpercollinschildrens.com